Candlelight

Story by Beverley Randell
Illustrations by Nathalie Ortega

"Ben, it's dinner time,"
said Mom, one wet night.

"I'm coming," said Ben.

Then, all the lights went out.

"Help! I can't see you," said Ben.

"I'm here by the window,"
said Mom.

Ben went to the window,
and he looked up the road
at the houses.
No one had a light on.
No one.

"Where did I put the candles?" said Mom.

"They are up there," said Ben.

"Good boy," said Mom.

They had dinner
in the yellow candlelight.

"I like candles," said Mom.

"Me too," said Ben.
"This is good fun."

At bedtime, Ben and Mom went into the bathroom with a candle. Ben sang a little song.

This is the way I brush my teeth,
I brush my teeth, I brush my teeth.
This is the way I brush my teeth,
I like my yellow candle.

They went into Ben's bedroom
with the candle . . .
but before he got into bed,
the lights came on!

"Oh, Mom!" said Ben.
"The lights have come on!
I **liked** my candle.
I don't want to turn it off."

Mom smiled,

and she put the lights out.

"You can have a candle,"

she said, and **she** sang a song.

Here comes a candle

to light you to bed,

*and here comes a **story***

for Ben and for Ted.

And then, after the story,

Mom turned the candle off.